The Sleepover Secret

Look for more

titles:
#1 *It's a Twin Thing*
#2 *How to Flunk Your First Date*

TWO of a kind ™

The Sleepover Secret

adapted by Judy Katschke

From the teleplay by Dan Cross and David Hoge

■ HarperEntertainment
A PARACHUTE PRESS BOOK

A PARACHUTE PRESS BOOK

Parachute Publishing, L.L.C.
156 Fifth Avenue
Suite 325
New York, NY 10010

Published by
HarperEntertainment
A Division of HarperCollins*Publishers*
10 East 53rd Street, New York, NY 10022-5299

For information, address HarperCollins Publishers,
10 East 53rd Street, New York, NY 10022-5299.

ISBN 0-06-106573-0

HarperCollins®, ™ ®, and HarperEntertainment™ are trademarks of
HarperCollins Publishers Inc.

First printing: March 1999

Printed in the United States of America

Visit HarperEntertainment on the World Wide Web at
http://www.harpercollins.com

10 9 8 7 6 5 4 3 2

CHAPTER ONE

"I just have one question," Mary-Kate Burke said. She unwrapped her peanut butter sandwich in the school lunchroom. "Why do they call them sleep-overs if nobody ever sleeps?"

Her twin sister, Ashley, ignored her. She was busy studying the list for her first sleepover of the school year.

"I stayed up all night at a sleepover once," their friend Amanda groaned. "The next day I was so tired, I brushed my teeth with sunblock!"

"Gross!" Ashley said. She ran her finger down the list and read the names out loud: "Darcy ... Melanie ... Rachel ... Amanda ... "

"Hey!" Max leaned over the table and stared at

1

the list. "Where's my name?"

"And what about mine?" another friend, Brian, asked.

Ashley looked at Max and Brian and shook her head. Why did she have to go through this every year?

"Guys," Ashley said. "You just don't get it, do you?"

Max took a long, loud slurp of his chocolate milk. Then he burped. "Get what?"

"You're boys," Mary-Kate pointed out. "If boys came to sleepovers there'd be nobody to trash!"

Max and Brian looked at each other and shrugged.

"No problem," Brian said coolly. "Because we guys just happen to have our own sleepovers, right, Max?"

"Yeah!" Max said. "We pitch tents in the back-yard, and see who can shove the most raisins up his nose."

Brian nodded. "Then we eat a load of barbecue chips and see who hurls first."

"Why am I not surprised?" Ashley groaned.

Mary-Kate took a sip of apple juice. "If I were you, I wouldn't worry. Knowing Ashley, you aren't the guys we'll be talking about at *this* sleepover."

"Oh, yeah?" Brian asked through a mouthful of pretzels. "Why not?"

Max slapped his forehead with the back of his hand. "Don't tell me—Ashley likes someone!"

Ashley shot Mary-Kate a look of warning.

"Mary-Kate," she whispered. "You better keep a lid on it . . . or else!"

"Okay, okay," Mary-Kate said. She turned to Amanda, Max, and Brian. "But I'll give you a little hint. To figure out who Ashley likes this week, just put two and two together."

"Two and two together?" Max repeated.

"What is this, some kind of math problem?" Brian asked.

"Math?" Amanda exclaimed, jumping up. "I know! I know!"

"Mary-Kate's math tutor—Taylor Donovan!" Amanda, Max, and Brian announced together.

"Arrrgh!" Ashley groaned. Thanks to her sister, the secret was out!

Ashley was just about to change the subject, when she heard the sound of giggles from across the lunchroom. She looked up and saw Jennifer Dilber and her friends sitting down at their own table—the cool table!

"Quick, Mary-Kate," Ashley whispered. She stuffed her peanut butter and jelly sandwich back in her lunch bag. Then she straightened her already neat purple cardigan over her black skirt. "Hide your sandwich before Jennifer and her friends see it."

"Why?" Mary-Kate asked.

"Because peanut butter is so . . . so kindergarten!" Ashley explained.

"No, it isn't!" Mary-Kate replied. She held her sandwich up in front of Ashley's face. "I like peanut butter. Besides, it's all Dad knows how to make without destroying the kitchen."

"Shhh," Ashley warned. "Jennifer might hear you."

Amanda wrinkled her nose. "What's so special about snooty Jennifer Dilber and her friends, anyway?" she asked.

"What's so special?" Ashley repeated. "Let me count the ways. . . ."

Everyone watched as Ashley tapped her fingertips.

"They have the coolest clothes. They get invited to the best parties . . . oh yeah, and they wear different colored rubber bands on their braces!"

"But can any of them throw a knuckleball?" Mary-Kate asked. She leaned over the table and gave Max a high-five.

Ashley shook her head at Mary-Kate and glanced back at Jennifer and her friends. She sighed.

"Look at them," she said. "They're all eating salads out of little plastic bowls. With real salad

4

dressing. That's pretty classy."

"You think so?" Mary-Kate said. "I bet deep inside they're all dying for a deluxe cheeseburger with fries!"

"Right on!" Max said with a grin.

"Ashley, if you think Jennifer is so great, why don't you invite her to your sleepover?" Mary-Kate asked.

Ashley gasped. "Are you serious?" Inviting Jennifer Dilber to her sleepover would be like inviting Madonna!

"Mary-Kate," Ashley said, "Jennifer wouldn't come to my sleepover in a million years. She and her friends don't even know I exist.

"Oh, yeah?" Mary-Kate snatched a grape from Amanda's sandwich bag. She grinned as she carefully aimed it toward Jennifer's table. "They will *now!*"

Ashley jumped up. "Mary-Kate! You wouldn't!" she pleaded.

Mary-Kate flicked the grape into the air. It soared through the lunchroom until it landed—right in the middle of the cool table!

Ashley held her breath as the grape rolled off the table into Jennifer's lap.

"Yes!" Mary-Kate cried. "A perfect pitch!"

"You go, girl!" Max cheered.

Jennifer and her friends turned and glared at

them. Ashley groaned. How could her sister do this to her?

"Here she comes," Brian declared as Jennifer stood up and walked toward them.

"And she looks maaa-aaad!" Max said.

Jennifer held the grape between her index finger and thumb.

"Does this belong to anyone?" she asked as she flicked the grape on the table.

"It does! Thanks, Jennifer!" Ashley grabbed the grape and stuffed it into Mary-Kate's mouth. "Slippery little rascal!"

"MMMMPH!" Mary-Kate gulped.

Jennifer folded her arms and wrinkled up her nose. "Is that peanut butter I smell?" she asked.

"Peanut butter?" Ashley cried. She threw back her head and laughed. "No way. It's a special peanut sauce that I like to pour over my . . . um—"

"Jelly," Mary-Kate filled in.

Ashley kicked Mary-Kate under the table. Then she saw Jennifer reach for her sleepover list.

"What's this?" Jennifer asked, raising one eyebrow. "A sleepover party?"

Ashley held her breath as Jennifer looked up and down the list.

"There isn't a sleepover in Chicago that I'm not

invited to," Jennifer said, still studying the paper.

Ashley's heart skipped a beat.

"Oh, you wouldn't want to come to my sleepover, Jennifer," she said, trying to sound casual.

"Yeah," Mary-Kate agreed. She shrugged. "We don't have the slightest idea how to make strawberry popcorn."

"Who says I wouldn't want to come?" Jennifer snapped.

The lunch table fell silent.

Ashley's jaw dropped. Did she just hear what she thought she heard? Did Jennifer Dilber, the queen of cool, just say she'd come to *Ashley's* sleepover?

"Excuse me?" Ashley said in a tiny voice.

"I was supposed to go to Danielle Frobisher's sleepover this Friday night," Jennifer explained. "But her little brother has chicken pox."

"Bummer," Max said.

"I'll say." Jennifer groaned. "A Friday night without a sleepover will ruin my reputation!"

Ashley almost fell off her seat. "D-does that mean you'll come?" she asked.

"I guess," Jennifer said. She looked bored. "But if you want me to come to your sleepover you have to follow my rules."

"Oh, brother!" Mary-Kate muttered under her breath.

"Sure, Jennifer," Ashley said. She gave Mary-Kate a poke. "What?"

"There'll be no scary stories in the dark," Jennifer declared firmly.

"Why not?" Amanda asked.

Jennifer flipped her long hair over her shoulder. "Because that is so *totally* sixth grade. Now that we're in seventh grade, we'll put on makeup and call some boys."

"That's not scary?" Mary-Kate cried.

"Sounds cool, Jennifer." Ashley's hands shook as she scribbled her address on a piece of paper.

"The sleepover starts at seven tomorrow night," she said. "Just bring your own sleeping bag and a toothbrush."

Jennifer gave a little snicker. "I *know* what to bring, Ashley. As if I've never been to a sleepover before."

Ashley watched Jennifer flip her hair and walk back to her table. She grabbed Mary-Kate's arm and began to shake it.

"Jennifer Dilber is coming to my sleepover!" Ashley squealed. "I can't believe I did it!"

Max jerked his head towards Mary-Kate.

"I think it was Mary-Kate's grape that did it," he said.

Mary-Kate picked up another grape. She held

it lovingly and sighed. "Food fights. A little messy at first, but in the end, they always bring people together."

Max and Brian grunted in agreement.

Ashley barely heard them. She was so excited, she couldn't finish her lunch.

She was about to start a new life—as a totally cool girl!

CHAPTER TWO

"Well, so much for toasting marshmallows in the microwave," Mary-Kate said that afternoon, after school. She reached into the microwave and pulled out a plate of drippy marshmallow goo.

"Although they did turn a nice golden brown just before they exploded," Carrie Moore said. She scooped up some of the sticky goo and ate it. "I guess we better not mention this to your dad."

"It's a deal," Mary-Kate giggled.

Carrie was Mary-Kate and Ashley's regular after-school baby-sitter. Their mother died when they were eight. In the three years since then, they'd had lots of baby-sitters. But Carrie was different from the others. She liked to have fun—even if it meant blowing up the whole kitchen!

Mary-Kate was about to stick her finger in the melted marshmallow goo when Ashley ran into the kitchen.

"Carrie, Carrie," she cried. "Guess what? I just got off the phone with Jennifer Dilber, and it's official!"

Carrie looked confused. "Official? What's official?"

"Jennifer's coming to my sleepover tomorrow night!" Ashley exclaimed. She began jumping up and down. "I didn't want to tell you until it was absolutely, positively definite!"

"Congratulations!" Carrie said. "That's so exciting! I can't believe Jennifer Dilber is coming." She frowned. "Who's Jennifer Dilber?"

Mary-Kate folded her arms across her chest. It was time to set the record straight.

"Only the most stuck-up girl in the seventh grade," she explained. "She has her own 'I Love Jennifer' Web page. You'll find it at 'gag dot com.'"

Ashley stuck her chin out at Mary-Kate. "You're just jealous because I'm becoming friends with the most popular girl in school!"

"It's tearing me up inside!" Mary-Kate clutched her chest.

"Mary-Kate, this has *got* to be the best party ever," Ashley insisted as she paced back and forth.

11

"Starting with the snacks."

"That's easy," Mary-Kate said. "We already made a list, remember?"

"Forget *that* old list," Ashley said. She turned to Carrie. "Carrie, can you make strawberry popcorn?"

"Hel-lo?" Carrie pointed to the gloppy microwave. "I can't even roast marshmallows!"

"Okay," Ashley shrugged. "Then we'll have three different kinds of salads."

"Salads?" Mary-Kate cried. Now she knew her sister was losing it. "All that green stuff?"

"Don't worry," Carrie whispered. "You can sprinkle them with nacho chips."

"Okay, okay, we'll get back to the menu." Ashley tapped her chin. "Now—what are we going to do for fun?"

"It's a sleepover," Mary-Kate said. "You wait for someone to fall asleep, duct tape her to the floor, then tell her the house is on fire."

"I was asking *Carrie*," Ashley snapped.

"I don't know," Carrie said. "That duct tape thing sounds like fun to me."

"Carrie, I'm serious!" Ashley threw up her hands. "If this party goes well, I could be eating at a whole new lunch table!"

"Okay, okay," Carrie said. "Since this is the social

event of the year, I'd say stick with the three F's. Food, facials, and . . . um . . . phone."

"Great!" Ashley declared. "We can call boys all night!"

"And say what?" Mary-Kate cried.

"Nothing," Ashley replied. "We wait until they answer and then we hang up."

"We used to do that at sleepovers when I was twelve," Carrie remembered.

"Okay. Let's get back to the food," Ashley reminded them. "We've got to come up with something better than Dad's cooking."

"What *about* my cooking?"

Mary-Kate spun around. Whoops! There was their dad, coming through the door with an armload of groceries.

"Oh, hi, Dad!" Mary-Kate said quickly. She wiped her sticky hands on a dish towel. "We were just talking about those great peanut butter sandwiches you made for us today."

"Funny that you mention peanut butter." Kevin Burke smiled. "When I was at the supermarket, I thought I'd start varying your lunches from now on."

"Varying?" Ashley repeated hopefully.

"As in . . . change?" Mary-Kate asked.

Maybe make-your-own pizzas, she thought. *Or better*

yet—make-your-own tacos!

Kevin nodded. He reached into the bag and pulled out two jars of peanut butter. "Smooth . . . and super chunky!"

"Gee, thanks, Dad," Ashley mumbled.

Mary-Kate stood on her toes to peek into the bag. "Did you remember to pick up the snacks on our list?" she asked.

"Well, your handwriting was a little smudged," Kevin said. "I couldn't tell whether you wanted corn chips or corn pads."

"Oh, no!" Ashley put her hand to her forehead. She looked horrified. "Say it isn't so!"

Kevin put his hand on Ashley's trembling shoulder. "Ashley, I was only kidding."

Ashley glared at him. "Dad, don't joke," she said. "One bad sleepover and I'll be eating lunch with the science nerds."

Carrie cleared her throat. "Your dad *teaches* science, Ashley," she said. Carrie was in Kevin's environmental studies class at the local college.

"Whoops," Ashley said quickly. "No offense, Dad."

"Ashley's losing it, Dad." Mary-Kate shook her head. "Big-time."

"She's just excited, Professor," Carrie explained. "Jennifer Dilber is coming to the party."

14

"Oooh!" Kevin said. He gave a low bow. "Jennifer Dilber! Royalty!"

"Yeah," Mary-Kate muttered. "A royal pain!"

Ashley ignored Mary-Kate. She began pulling food out of the grocery bag and placing it on the counter.

"Ice cream, M&M's . . . *baloney?*" Ashley shrieked. Her hand shook as she held the package. "I can't feed Jennifer Dilber baloney!"

Kevin grabbed the package out of Ashley's hand. "That's my lunch for tomorrow."

"Well, it should be in a separate bag," Ashley insisted. "People—help me out here!"

"Get a grip!" Mary-Kate groaned under her breath. She had a sinking feeling it was a mistake to invite Jennifer Dilber to the sleepover.

There are two possibilities here, she thought. *Either this sleepover will be the best party we've ever had—or it will be a disaster.*

I'm betting on the disaster.

CHAPTER THREE

"I know this was a tough test," Kevin said, as his students filed out of the classroom the next day. "But remember, you get to throw out your lowest score."

One of the students, Paul Gundry, stopped at Kevin's desk. He crumpled up his test paper.

"Paul, Paul," Kevin said. He reached out his hand to stop him. "I meant, after I grade them!"

"Oh," Paul said. He dropped the paper back on the desk. "Sorry about that."

Kevin watched his class leave. They looked worried about the test. He knew how they felt. He was worried, too, but not about crystals and ions. He was worried about Ashley's sleepover tonight.

I can barely handle two eleven-year-old girls, Kevin

thought. *How in the world am I going to handle eight?*

All his students had left except for Carrie. He watched her scribble a final answer on her test page.

"This is it, Professor!" Carrie smiled as she placed the paper on his desk. "I know I didn't do so great on the last test, but I'm pretty sure I aced this one!"

"I wouldn't be surprised," Kevin said. He knew Carrie had dropped out of college and was back again after seven years. "After all that time away from school, you're finally getting into the swing of it."

"Finally!" Carrie agreed. She gave a little salute and walked toward the door.

Kevin started to panic. She couldn't go yet!

"Wait, Carrie," he called. "Are you doing anything tonight?"

Carrie turned around and shrugged.

"Just the usual, Professor," she replied. "Eat, drink, and be Carrie."

"Cute," Kevin said. "Well, how would you feel about going to Ashley's sleepover?"

"It all depends." Carrie pretended to consider. "Do I get to paint my toenails and call some boys?"

"No, Carrie," Kevin said. "You'd be working."

"Working?" Carrie repeated.

Kevin nodded. "I, uh, I get the feeling Ashley doesn't actually want me there."

"How do you know?" Carrie asked.

"She *said* so," Kevin admitted.

"Oh, in that case," Carrie said, "I'd be happy to come over. I've got plenty of fun ideas for a sleepover."

Kevin was almost afraid to ask.

"What kind of fun ideas?"

"Sundaes," Carrie suggested. "Mounds and mounds of gooey ice cream sundaes. With hot fudge and marshmallows."

"Sundaes, huh?" Kevin smiled.

"Why not?" Carrie said. "We already have the marshmallow sauce!"

Marshmallow sauce?

Kevin's mouth dropped open.

"So that's what was oozing out of the microwave!" he exclaimed.

Carrie gave a little shrug.

Kevin looked at the clock on his wall. It was already two o'clock. Five hours left to Operation Sleepover!

"Carrie," he said, "I'd like you to be there at seven o'clock sharp."

Carrie held up her hand. "Stop. First things first. You are going to pay me extra, right?"

"Whatever it takes." Kevin nodded. "And you don't mind the couch, do you?"

"It's a nice couch," Carrie said. She moved toward the door. "But I'd really prefer cash. See you tonight at seven."

"See you," Kevin called. "And thanks again."

Kevin watched Carrie leave. He pumped his fist in the air. "Ye-es!" he cheered.

With Carrie there, Ashley's sleepover will be smooth sailing all the way, he thought. *A harmless, innocent night of ghost stories and sundaes with marshmallow sauce.*

He was prepared.

He had everything under control.

What could possibly go wrong?

CHAPTER FOUR

"Oh, Jennifer!" Ashley gushed. "That shade of blush makes you look so . . . so mature!"

Jennifer pulled the blush brush away from her face. She sucked in her cheeks and stared in the handheld mirror. "It's called the natural look!"

Mary-Kate stood up and tugged at her oversize Chicago Cubs T-shirt. "Natural? You've been glopping that stuff on your face for the last hour!"

Ashley squeezed her eyes shut. *Please, Mary-Kate! Don't ruin my sleepover—please!*

"Mary-Kate," Ashley said sharply, "some things are worth the wait."

Mary-Kate pointed to the clock on the wall. "But we could have made at least ten crank calls by now!"

That does it, Ashley thought. *Time out.*

She stood up and dragged her sister to the corner of the attic.

"What?" Mary-Kate asked.

"Mary-Kate!" Ashley whispered. "Would it kill you to act cool for just one night? One night—that's all I'm asking you!"

Mary-Kate pointed to Jennifer and the other girls. "If that's acting cool, I'd rather blow up aliens!"

"Blow up aliens?" Ashley repeated.

Mary-Kate sat down on the floor. She picked up her *Morons from Mars* video game and began to play.

"Fine," Ashley muttered.

She straightened her silky pink pajamas and looked around the attic. She and Mary-Kate used it as their private hangout. The floor was covered with sleeping bags, bowls of snacks, and piles of clothes.

So far so good.

"Go on with your makeup demonstration, Jennifer," Ashley urged.

"I will," Jennifer said. She glanced over her shoulder. "As soon as Amanda gets out of my light."

"Amanda!" Ashley exclaimed, horrified. "Get out of Jennifer's light!"

"Okay, okay," Amanda wiggled over to where Mary-Kate was sitting. "Don't bite my head off."

Ashley and her friends Darcy and Melanie watched as Jennifer put the final touches on her freshly made-up face.

"Tah-daaah!" Jennifer sang as she put down the mirror.

Ashley stared at Jennifer. Her eyelids were painted a bright lavender that matched her glossy lips. Two streaks of pink were smudged across her cheeks. And her eyebrows were two shades darker than her hair!

Jennifer put the mirror down. "And this, girls, is how Salon Jeffrey did my makeover when my mother took me to New York!"

Waving her arms, Ashley led the girls in a chorus of ooohs and ahhhs.

"Of course, none of you should expect results like this," Jennifer warned.

"Of course not!" Ashley agreed. She could hear Mary-Kate and Amanda snickering in the background.

"Mary-Kate, is it me or does Jennifer look a bit overdone?" Amanda whispered loudly.

"Not if she's planning to join the circus," Mary-Kate replied.

"I heard that, Mary-Kate," Jennifer snapped.

Ashley held her breath. But Jennifer didn't say anything more. She simply placed her brushes, cases, and bottles into a plastic daisy-print bag. The demonstration was over.

"What should we do now, Jennifer?" Ashley asked.

Jennifer grinned. "I think it's time we called some boys."

"Good idea," Ashley said. "I'll get the phone book."

"I don't need a phone book." Jennifer smiled. She reached over to her knapsack and pulled out a small hot-pink book. "I have all the numbers I want right here."

"Who should we call?" Darcy asked.

Jennifer didn't answer. She just picked up the phone and held it out to Ashley.

"Ashley," Jennifer said, "I'm going to dial Greg Garcia. But I want you to talk to him."

Ashley felt a huge lump in her throat.

"Talk?" she gulped.

Jennifer rolled her eyes. "What else do you do when you call a boy?" she asked.

Ashley shrugged. "Hang up?"

"Like we always do at sleepovers," Amanda explained.

Jennifer gave a big sigh as she looked at the clock. "You know . . . Danielle Frobisher's brother is probably not even contagious. And I've already had the chicken pox. Maybe I can still talk her into having a sleepover."

Oh, no! Ashley thought. *Jennifer can't leave—she just can't!*

"I was only kidding about hanging up." Ashley grabbed the phone. "But Greg Garcia? Why do you want me to call that geek anyhow?"

"Because everyone knows I have a crush on him," Jennifer said sharply.

Ashley froze.

"Oh, *that* Greg Garcia!" she said quickly. "He's a great guy!"

"His number is 555-2613." Jennifer smiled. "I know that one by heart."

Ashley tried to look confident as she pushed the buttons on the phone pad.

"This I've got to hear," Mary-Kate muttered as she wiggled over to her twin.

"Is it ringing?" Jennifer whispered.

Ashley nodded. The phone was ringing—but her knees were knocking. The only boys she ever called were Max and Brian. And they didn't count.

"What are you going to say first?" Amanda asked.

"Yeah." Melanie giggled. "What are you going to say?"

Okay, Ashley thought nervously. *Act as if you've done this over a hundred times.*

"I thought I'd start with, 'hey,' " Ashley said.

"That's perfect," Jennifer said.

"Yeah," Mary-Kate agreed, "because 'hi' is so sixth grade!"

Ashley shot her sister a look of warning. This call was the ultimate test. If it came off without a hitch, she would earn Jennifer Dilber's respect. She would—

"Hello?" a woman on the other end of the phone said.

"H-hi," Ashley stammered. "Mrs. Garcia?"

"Yes?" Mrs. Garcia answered.

Ashley took a deep breath. "Is . . . Greg . . . there?"

"Yes," Mrs. Garcia said. "But he's in the shower now."

Saved! Ashley thought.

"Would you like to leave a message?" Ms. Garcia asked.

"No!" Ashley said quickly. "Thanks, bye."

Ashley felt her heart pound as she hung up. Glancing up, she saw that all eyes were on her.

"Well?" Jennifer demanded. "What happened?"

The other girls leaned forward for Ashley's answer.

"His mom said he was in the shower," Ashley said coolly.

The attic grew silent as the girls stared at each

other. Then they all shrieked with laughter.

"Taking a shower!" Amanda gasped. "That's so cool!"

"Well, at least we know he's clean!" Melanie joked.

"Which boy are we calling next?" Darcy asked excitedly.

"We're not," Jennifer said.

"What do you mean?" Ashley asked.

"After Greg Garcia it's all downhill as far as I'm concerned," Jennifer replied. "Let's play a game instead."

"Now you're talking!" Mary-Kate exclaimed, jumping up. "We have Clue, Monopoly, and a very scary Ouija board."

Jennifer shook her head. "I don't think so."

"Then what do you want to play, Jennifer?" Ashley asked.

Jennifer tilted her head as she looked at each girl one by one.

"How about a round of . . . Truth or Dare?"

CHAPTER FIVE

"Truth or Dare?" Ashley repeated.

"Oh, great," Mary-Kate grumbled. She hated Truth or Dare! Jennifer smiled. "Is everyone in?"

Mary-Kate watched as Ashley's friends nodded slowly.

"Sure, Jennifer," Ashley said cheerfully. "Let the game begin."

"Cool," Jennifer said. "Amanda goes first."

"Why me?" Amanda wailed.

"Alphabetical order," Jennifer explained.

"That means you're next," Mary-Kate whispered to Ashley.

All eyes were on Amanda as Jennifer spoke. "Okay, Amanda. Truth or dare?"

Amanda narrowed her eyes at Jennifer. "Dare."

"In that case . . . " Jennifer said. She looked around the attic and grabbed a bag of marshmallows. "I dare you to stick twenty marshmallows in your mouth!"

Mary-Kate gasped. Amanda hated marshmallows. This game was getting ugly—fast!

"Twenty?" Amanda shrieked. "I can't even stand marshmallows in my hot chocolate!"

Mary-Kate could see that Ashley was getting nervous. Almost as nervous as Amanda.

"Go for it, Amanda," Ashley urged.

"Yeah, Amanda, go ahead," Jennifer said. "Unless you want us to switch it to . . . brussels sprouts?"

"Eeeww!" the girls cried.

What's wrong with brussels sprouts? Mary-Kate thought. *I like brussels sprouts!*

"You win," Amanda muttered. She grabbed the first marshmallow and stuck it in her mouth. Then she made a face.

"One down," Jennifer said. "Nineteen to go."

Mary-Kate watched as Amanda stuck marshmallows in her mouth one by one. By the time she got up to sixteen, her cheeks were puffed out like a chipmunk's.

"Seventeen!" the girls chanted.

"How are you doing, Amanda?" Ashley asked.

How is she doing? Mary-Kate thought. *She's almost as green as Kermit the Frog!*

"Jushhhh fine," Amanda mumbled through a mouthful of puffs. She looked sick as she reached for another.

"Eighteen, nineteen, twenty!" the girls continued to chant.

"You did it, Amanda!" Ashley cried.

Mary-Kate saw Amanda's mouth blow up even larger.

"Whoa!" Mary-Kate cried. "Stand back, everybody. She's about to erupt!"

"Phoooooo!" Amanda puffed.

"There she blows!" Mary-Kate screamed. The girls shrieked as twenty soggy marshmallows flew through the attic. A few stuck to the ceiling while others bounced off the walls.

When the excitement died down, Jennifer pulled a clammy marshmallow from her hair.

"That was totally gross," she complained.

"You asked for it," Amanda said, slumped over. Her face was still greenish and sweaty. She wiped clumps of marshmallow from her chin as she turned to Ashley. "Okay, Ashley. Your turn."

Mary-Kate looked over at her sister. What would it be?

"Truth!" Ashley said with a smile.

Amanda gave it a thought. Then she grinned.

"Okay, Ashley," she said. "If you had to spend the rest of your life on a deserted island with only one boy, who would it be?"

"I like that question," Jennifer said. "Go ahead, Ashley. Who would it be?"

"Oh, that's easy," Ashley said. She gave Mary-Kate a little wink. "The answer is . . . Taylor Donovan."

"Who's Taylor Donovan?" Jennifer asked. She looked excited.

"My math tutor," Mary-Kate offered.

"He's fifteen," Ashley added. "He has his own band, and his cousin was on *Jeopardy!*"

"Fifteen?" Jamie squealed.

"An older guy!" Darcy gasped.

Mary-Kate looked around the attic. The girls seemed interested—except Jennifer. She just looked bored.

"A math tutor, huh? Okay, okay." Jennifer sighed. She pointed to Mary-Kate. "You're next, Mary-Kate."

"But my name begins with M!" Mary-Kate protested. "You go before I do!"

Ashley nudged her sister. "Just do it."

"No," Mary-Kate said. "I'm not playing."

"What's the matter?" Jennifer snickered. "Are you chicken? Cluck! Cluck! Cluck!"

Mary-Kate glared at Jennifer. No way would she let Miss High-and-Mighty make her look like a wimp!

"Fine!" Mary-Kate snapped. "Truth."

"This is going to be good," Jennifer said. She rubbed her hands together. "Mary-Kate? What's the most you ever did with a boy?"

The sound of ooohs and woos filled the attic.

So she wants the truth, huh? Mary-Kate thought. *Okay—I'll give her the truth. Let's see if she can handle it!*

"All right, all right," Mary-Kate said. "This year . . . at the Fourth of July picnic . . . I kissed a boy!"

CHAPTER SIX

"You *what?*" Ashley gasped.

"I kissed a boy," Mary-Kate repeated with a shrug.

"On the lips?" Amanda shrieked.

"Uh-huh," Mary-Kate said.

"You did not, Mary-Kate," Ashley said. "You're making the whole thing up!"

"No, I'm not," Mary-Kate said. "Cross my heart and hope to get a fungus between my toes."

This can't be happening, Ashley thought. *Mary-Kate is my twin. We share everything—a birthday, a bedroom, and all our secrets!*

"How come you never told me?" Ashley demanded.

"Because you can't keep a secret," Mary-Kate said.

"I can't keep a secret?" Ashley cried. "You're the

one who told the lunch table I liked Taylor Donovan!"

This is an absolute nightmare, Ashley thought. *I'm two minutes older than Mary-Kate. And she kissed a boy already? I never kissed a boy!*

"So who was it?" Jennifer urged.

"Gary Goodrich," Mary-Kate answered.

Jennifer's eyes lit up. "You kissed Gary Goodrich? I heard he kissed someone at the Fourth of July picnic. What was it like?"

"It was a blast," Mary-Kate said. "Now can we play Clue?"

"No!" Jennifer protested. "I want details!"

Ashley watched in horror as her friends circled around Mary-Kate. Suddenly her sister was the star of the party!

"Okay." Mary-Kate sighed. "I kept my eyes open but he kept his closed."

"What a man!" Amanda cried.

"Go on, Mary-Kate," Jennifer urged. "Tell us more!"

Ashley felt beads of sweat on her forehead. This was her sleepover, not Mary-Kate's!

Maybe if she changed the subject.

"The worst part of the whole thing," Mary-Kate went on, "was that he was chewing on a big — "

"Pizza?" Ashley said quickly.

The girls turned and stared at her.

"Huh?" Jennifer asked, annoyed.

"Would anyone like me to order a pizza?" Ashley asked sweetly.

The girls shook their heads, and Mary-Kate continued.

"He was still chewing on a piece of nacho chip," Mary-Kate said. "So his whole mouth smelled like—"

"Pepperoni?" Ashley chirped.

"What?" Jennifer cried.

"Should I order mushrooms . . . or pepperoni?" Ashley asked, desperately.

"Whatever." Jennifer sighed. "Go on, Mary-Kate."

"Anyway," Mary-Kate continued. "He had nacho-breath. But at least he wasn't wearing braces—"

Ashley felt her heart sink as she dialed the pizza parlor. Mary-Kate kept a major secret from her, and now she was stealing her party—and her friends!

How could Mary-Kate do this to me? she wondered. *How?*

CHAPTER SEVEN

"It's so quiet upstairs," Kevin said to Carrie. He sat down on the living room sofa. "Do you think they're okay?"

Carrie smiled at Kevin. He was definitely suffering from worried-dad syndrome!

"I don't know," she replied. "Maybe they snuck out, stole your car, and are cruising for a place to buy chocolate donuts."

A sudden roar of laughter erupted upstairs. Carrie watched Kevin sigh with relief.

"I guess they're back," Carrie joked.

"I'm not paying you to make fun of me," Kevin said.

"I know," Carrie said. "I threw that in for free."

She sat on the sofa next to Kevin. She studied him

out of the corner of her eye. They'd spent the whole evening making ice cream sundaes and cheese dip. Now it was time to get down to business. . . .

"So, Professor," Carrie said, "I'm guessing you finished grading the tests we took today."

Kevin nodded. "Most of them."

Carrie held her breath as she waited for a sign on the professor's face. Any sign that would tell her if she aced the test . . . or blew it!

"It would be nice to know how I did, so I could enjoy the rest of my weekend," Carrie said slowly.

"Well, Carrie," Kevin said. "I did grade your test. And I'm happy to say that . . . "

Carrie sat up on the sofa. "Yeah? Yeah?"

"You'll find out next week like everyone else," Kevin finished.

Carrie leaned back on the sofa and moaned. She picked up a pillow and shook it. "When is this whole 'working for the professor' thing going to pay off?" she asked.

The doorbell rang.

"Who could that be?" Kevin wondered out loud. He stood up and walked to the front door.

Curious, Carrie followed Kevin. She watched as he opened the door.

"Got an extra large supreme with everything," she

heard a familiar voice say.

"Paul?" Kevin asked.

Carrie grinned. It was Paul Gundry—college student by day, pizza delivery boy by night. He was in her science class with Professor Burke.

"Professor?" Paul said. "Wow, small world."

"I didn't order a pizza," Kevin said, confused.

"You didn't?" Paul asked. "Then who did?"

Carrie turned her eyes to the attic and smiled. She had a pretty good idea who did.

"I think I know, Professor," Carrie said, joining Kevin at the door. "One cannot live on ice cream sundaes alone, you know."

Paul's mouth dropped wide open. "Carrie? What are you doing here?"

"Hi, Paul," Carrie said with a smile. She reached out and grabbed the pizza box.

"I-I-I," Paul stammered. He looked at Kevin. Then at Carrie. Then at Kevin again.

Uh-oh. Carrie didn't have to be a mind reader to know what her classmate was thinking. He thought she and Kevin were on a date!

"Okay, Paul," Kevin mumbled as he nervously reached for his wallet. "I know this looks bad."

Paul grinned from ear to ear. "Looks great to me, Professor. Enjoy your pizza!"

"Wait, Paul," Kevin called as Paul jumped on his bike. "I can explain!"

But it was too late. Paul was gone.

Kevin looked helplessly at Carrie. "Paul thinks I . . . I mean . . . he thinks you and I—"

"I know," Carrie said. She sighed.

Paul thinks that I'm dating Kevin, she thought. *But I'm not, so I'm not going to worry about what he thinks.*

And it's really none of his business anyhow. It's my business.

Isn't it?

CHAPTER
EIGHT

"Awesome party, Mary-Kate," Amanda said the next morning. She smiled and gave Mary-Kate two thumbs up.

Mary-Kate? It was my party! My party! Ashley thought as her guests filed out the door with their sleeping bags.

"Thanks, Amanda," Mary-Kate said.

"You're definitely coming to my next sleepover," Melanie declared, balancing her sleeping bag under one arm.

Mary-Kate raised a finger. "Don't lock me in just yet. I have a very busy social schedule, you know."

Ashley watched sadly as her friends waved good-bye to Mary-Kate. Just twenty-four hours ago she

39

was the popular one. What a difference a day made—
a day and a stupid kiss!

"Thanks, Mary-Kate," Jennifer said on her way
out. "I'll see you in school on Monday. Hey—maybe
you can sit at our table for lunch!"

Ashley ran over to the door.

"Bye, Jennifer!" she said eagerly.

Jennifer glanced over her shoulder as she walked
down the stoop. Then she yawned.

"Oh . . . bye, Ashley," she said.

"Thanks for coming!" Ashley called. "And thanks
for bringing your makeup. I really learned a lot about
shading and coloring!"

Ashley watched Jennifer walk away. Then she
closed the door.

"Well," Mary-Kate said with a shrug. "I guess the
party's over."

"I hate you!" Ashley burst out.

Mary-Kate blinked a couple of times. "Why?"

"You ruined my party!" Ashley exclaimed.
"Telling everyone you kissed a boy. After you did
that, that's all they wanted to talk about!"

"What's the big deal?" Mary-Kate asked. "It's not
like I even liked the kiss. Gary had nacho breath."

Ashley folded her arms across her chest. "Oh, you
liked it, all right. If you didn't, you wouldn't have

kept talking about it for the whole night!"

"Can I help it if nobody wanted to play Twister?" Mary-Kate asked, waving her arms in the air. "Besides, they kept asking me for details. If Gary put his arms around me— "

Ashley held her hand up. "Spare me!"

"What is your problem?" Mary-Kate asked.

"I'll tell you what my problem is," Ashley shot back. "Now my friends like you better than they like me. Jennifer Dilber likes you better than me!"

"She'll get over it." Mary-Kate shrugged. "As soon as she finds out I like softball better than the mall."

"Maybe *she'll* get over it," Ashley said. "But I won't!"

"How come?" Mary-Kate asked.

Ashley stared at her sister. Did she really have to ask?

"You kept a big *secret* from me, Mary-Kate," Ashley said. "I never kept a secret from you."

"Oh, yeah?" Mary-Kate put her hands on her hips. "How about the time you snuck my loose tooth out from under my pillow and stuck it under yours? So you could get an extra buck from the tooth fairy?"

"Mary-Kate, we were five and a half years old!" Ashley cried. "Besides, kissing a boy is much more serious."

"Not if you're the tooth fairy," Mary-Kate replied.

Ashley let out a big sigh. "You just don't get it, do

you, Mary-Kate? My whole life is ruined—totally ruined! And it's all your fault."

"*Your* life is ruined?" Mary-Kate asked. "What about me? I'll never eat another nacho again!"

"Ooooh!" Ashley cried, spinning around. She ran toward the staircase and almost bumped into Carrie.

"Whoa!" Carrie said. She shifted her overnight bag on her shoulder. "Did I just hear Mary-Kate say she doesn't like nachos?"

Ashley glared at her sister.

"Yeah, but she doesn't have to worry," she replied coldly. "From now on she'll be eating alfalfa sprouts and mushrooms with Jennifer Dilber!"

CHAPTER NINE

Kevin gazed out at his class on Monday morning. He could feel Paul's eyes on him.

"Okay," Kevin began. He drew a crystal on the board and pointed to it. "Does anyone remember how ions attract one another?"

There was a long moment of silence. Then Paul leaned over to his friend Brett and whispered loudly.

"They order a late-night pizza!"

I heard that, Kevin thought. *But I'll—I'll just pretend I didn't!*

"Nobody?" Kevin said. "They're attracted to ions of the opposite charge."

From the corner of his eye, Kevin could see Paul and Brett whispering again.

Calm down, he thought. *Carrie and I didn't do anything wrong. We made ice cream sundaes and melted cheese on crackers.*

"Now, let's talk about what happens after the ions bond," Kevin went on.

"They finish their pizza and bond again!" Brett snickered.

Snorting with laughter, Paul and Brett exchanged high fives.

"Fine, that's it." Kevin threw up his hands. "You want to talk about it, let's talk about it."

All eyes were on Kevin as he cleared his throat.

"Obviously Paul told you that Carrie and I had a date on Friday night," Kevin said.

"Cool!" a student cried.

"Way to go, Professor Burke!" another student said.

"Actually, Professor Burke," Paul spoke up, "I only told Brett."

Kevin's mouth felt as dry as cotton. Especially with his foot in it!

"It was completely innocent," Kevin explained quickly. "Carrie was there for a sleepover. I couldn't handle so many girls alone—"

The class broke into roars of laughter.

"Carrie is my baby-sitter!" Kevin called out over

the laughs. He turned to Carrie and smiled. "Carrie, bail me out here, will you?"

Leaning back in her chair, Carrie twirled her pen in her hand.

"Go ahead, Carrie," Kevin urged. "Tell the class that we didn't have a date."

Carrie gave a little shrug. "No comment."

"No comment?" Kevin stared at Carrie. "What do you mean, no comment?"

"It's no one's business what I do in my personal life," Carrie explained.

No one's business? Kevin thought. *It's my business! Everyone knows that professors shouldn't date their students!*

He turned to Carrie and frowned. "Carrie, thank you for clearing everything up."

"No problem, Professor," Carrie answered.

"Now, getting back to crystals," Kevin said. He stared at the blackboard but couldn't remember what he wanted to say.

"Look," he said at last, turning to the class. "That's enough for today, okay?"

Students began heading for the door. As he gathered his papers, Kevin could hear his students whispering about him and Carrie.

"Um . . . Professor Burke?" Paul stopped at his desk.

"Yes, Paul?" Kevin said, not looking up.

"This isn't going to affect my grade, is it?" Paul asked.

Kevin sighed. "Good-bye, Paul."

As Paul and Brett left the classroom, Kevin saw Carrie stroll by. He ran around the desk and stopped her.

"And what was that all about?" he snapped. "Why didn't you help me out?"

Carrie straightened her shoulders. "Because I'm not going to defend myself against stupid gossip and rumors. I don't care what they think. Why should you, Professor Burke?"

"Because I do not date my students," Kevin explained. "And I don't want people thinking that I do."

Carrie stared down at her platform sandals.

"This university is like a small town," Kevin went on. "Rumors spread quickly here."

Carrie looked up and smiled. "Come on, Professor. What difference does it make what I say?"

"What?" Kevin asked.

"Everyone will just believe what they want to believe," Carrie said. "It's human nature. As a science professor you should know that!"

"I do know that," Kevin admitted. "But you still should have told everyone that we didn't have a date. You should have told them the truth."

"Look," Carrie said, "*we* know it wasn't a date. All we did was make ice cream sundaes and open up a few bags of chips!"

"Yeah," Kevin agreed."But *they* don't know that. You might think you don't care what people think, but rumors can have a way of backfiring."

He sighed.

"You'll see."

CHAPTER TEN

"Hey, Ashley," Mary-Kate said. She opened her lunch bag and pulled out a plastic-wrapped sandwich. "I'm happy to announce that we don't have peanut butter and jelly today. We have peanut butter and . . . bananas!"

Ashley looked gloomily down at her sandwich. She was still upset with Mary-Kate. Her sleepover was a disaster. It totally ruined her whole weekend—and her appetite.

"Hmmm?" she asked coolly. "Did you just say something, Mary-Kate?"

Mary-Kate tossed her sandwich down on the lunch table.

"Okay, Ashley," she said. She took a deep breath.

"Just how far do you want to take this?"

"What do you mean?" Ashley asked.

"I mean that we're twins!" Mary-Kate exclaimed. Her voice quivered. "We've known each other since we were born—even *before* we were born. Doesn't that mean *anything* to you?"

Ashley took a long sip of her cranberry juice. Mary-Kate sounded really upset. Maybe she had a point. Mary-Kate was her sister and her best friend. It was kind of dumb to fight over a sleepover.

"You're right, Mary-Kate." Ashley sighed. "Maybe I did kind of lose it."

Mary-Kate smiled in relief. "Kind of."

"Besides," Ashley went on, "nothing's really changed since my sleepover. We still live in the same house, go to the same school, and eat the same lunches—"

"Hi."

Ashley glanced up. Jennifer Dilber was standing over their table. She was wearing a tight ribbed sweater and baggy jeans.

"Hey, Jen," Mary-Kate said. "What's up?"

"Hi, Jennifer," Ashley said.

"Hi, Mary-Kate . . . Ashley," Jennifer said. She looked up and down the table. "Where's Amanda?"

"She's getting frozen yogurts with Max and

49

Brian," Ashley said. "Do you want to sit with us, Jennifer? There're plenty of chairs."

"No, thanks," Jennifer said. "Mary-Kate, will you come over to our table?"

Ashley's stomach did a triple flip.

"Who, me?" Mary-Kate asked.

"Sure," Jennifer said. "We're making a list of the cutest boys in school, and we'd like your opinion."

Mary-Kate's opinion? Ashley thought. *Since when is she an expert?*

"That's cool," Mary-Kate said. "But if it's okay with you, I'd like to stay here with my sister. We just started our sandwiches, right, Ashley?"

Ashley smiled at her sister and nodded. What a pal! She took a big bite of her peanut butter sandwich.

"Sandwiches? Are you for real?" Jennifer laughed. "Stacey Montrose brought in a whole container full of tacos!"

Mary-Kate's eyes lit up. "Did you say . . . tacos?"

Uh-oh, Ashley thought. *Mary-Kate never turned down a good taco in her whole life!*

"With salsa?" Mary-Kate asked slowly.

"Extra spicy." Jennifer nodded.

"Okay, I'll go for it," Mary-Kate decided. She turned to Ashley. "Want a taco, Ashley?"

"No, thanks," Ashley snapped.

Shrugging, Mary-Kate stood up and followed Jennifer to her table—the cool table!

I can't believe it! Ashley thought. *First Mary-Kate keeps a major secret from me. Then she takes over my sleepover. And now she's eating at the cool table—without me!*

Ashley felt a huge lump grow in her throat. And this time it wasn't from the peanut butter!

CHAPTER ELEVEN

"I can't believe I have to wake *you* up!" Mary-Kate said the next morning. She shook Ashley a couple of times until she groaned.

"Leave me alone," Ashley mumbled. She slipped deeper under her pink flowered quilt. "I want to sleep for a hundred years. Or more!"

"You mean, like Sleeping Beauty?" Mary-Kate said. "Cool. Then maybe some prince will come along and—"

Ashley threw back her comforter and glared at her sister. "Don't even say it. Don't even say the word *kiss!*"

Mary-Kate shook her head.

Things between her and Ashley had become a lot

worse since yesterday. She should never have gone to eat at the cool lunch table! Now Ashley either snapped at her—or she wouldn't speak to her at all.

"You know, Ashley," Mary-Kate joked, "if you don't get out of bed, it might just take you a hundred years to kiss a boy!"

Ashley grabbed her pillow and threw it at Mary-Kate. It landed on her chest with a thump.

Mary-Kate tossed the pillow on the floor. She looked around the bedroom they shared. Ashley's part of the room was usually super neat. But the last few days it had gotten almost as messy as Mary-Kate's!

"By the way," Mary-Kate said. She pulled on a gray sweatshirt over her jeans. "I won't be in the lunchroom today."

Ashley sat up in bed.

"You won't?" she asked. "Why not?"

"I promised Ms. Lang, the art teacher, I'd help her hang up paintings," Mary-Kate explained. "It's an extra-credit thing."

Ashley jumped out of bed.

"Um . . . Mary-Kate?" she said. "Can I borrow your Cubs T-shirt? And your jeans with the holes in the knees?"

Mary-Kate looked at Ashley as if she had three heads.

"Sure," she said slowly. "But didn't you always say my clothes were a disaster?"

Ashley threw back her head and laughed.

"I was just kidding," she explained. "Besides, I'm tired of thinking about clothes all the time. From now on, comfort comes first!"

Wait a minute, Mary-Kate thought. *Something's not right. Ashley wouldn't be caught dead wearing my clothes. Especially in front of Jennifer.*

Then she got it.

"Aha!" she cried. "I know what you're doing, Ashley!"

Ashley slipped her feet into her fuzzy slippers. "What do you mean?" she asked.

"You want to wear my clothes so the kids in the lunchroom will think that you're me!" Mary-Kate accused.

"Why would I want to do that?" Ashley asked.

Mary-Kate looked her sister straight in the eye. "So you can sit at the cool table," she said. "That's why."

Ashley plopped down on the bed. "Busted!" she muttered.

Mary-Kate opened her drawer. She pulled out her

Cubs T-shirt and her torn jeans. Then she tossed them onto Ashley's bed.

"Go ahead." She sighed. "If it's that important to you, wear my clothes."

Ashley picked up the holey jeans with two fingers. She looked down at the faded Cubs T-shirt.

Then she broke down.

"I . . . I . . . can't!" Ashley wailed.

"Look, Ashley," Mary-Kate said. "Why do you have to pretend that you're me, anyway? Why don't you just go over to Jennifer's table and be yourself?"

"Because you kissed a boy and I didn't!" Ashley declared.

Mary-Kate felt terrible.

Why did she have to play Truth or Dare?

And why didn't she pick dare instead? Sticking fifty raisins up her nose would have been better than this! She couldn't stand having Ashley angry with her.

She decided to try to make up one more time.

"I have an idea, Ashley," Mary-Kate suggested. "Why don't we both hang up paintings during lunch? I'll probably need some help."

"Help?" Ashley asked. "You didn't need my help after the Fourth of July picnic! Or at the sleepover!

Or at Jennifer's table! Or—"

Mary-Kate sighed. "I'm out of here."

It was like having the same nightmare over and over again!

Would Ashley *ever* forgive her?

CHAPTER TWELVE

"What about him?" Amanda whispered to Mary-Kate as a teenage boy walked past the stoop.

Mary-Kate looked the boy up and down. He was wearing a short-sleeved shirt and pants that came above his ankles. Two pens stuck out of his shirt pocket.

"Not cool," Mary-Kate whispered back.

The girls waited a few seconds until another boy went by. He had a short buzz cut and a nose ring.

"How about him?" Amanda asked.

"*Too* cool!" Mary-Kate declared, shaking her head.

"I still don't get it, Mary-Kate," Amanda said. "Why is it so important for you to find a boy for Ashley to kiss?"

"Because Ashley is mad at me," Mary-Kate explained. "I ruined her sleepover. I kept a major secret from her. And I kissed a boy before she did."

She swallowed hard.

"I can't do anything about the first two, but maybe I can do something about the kiss," she said. "Ashley has to kiss a boy, too. That way things will be even between us. And maybe she'll talk to me again."

Mary-Kate leaned her elbows back on the stoop and sighed.

"It's the pits, Amanda," she said. "This afternoon I put on a T-shirt with a huge ketchup stain on it, and Ashley didn't say a word. She didn't even make gagging sounds like she usually does."

"Ashley Burke, fashion police?" Amanda exclaimed. "That is weird, Mary-Kate."

"And that's just *one* example," Mary-Kate grumbled. "She didn't even sit with me on the school bus this morning. I had to sit next to a first grade boy with a jar of bugs on his lap!"

"Eeww!" Amanda shuddered.

The girls sat silently for a few moments.

"The worst part is, I don't blame Ashley for being mad at me," Mary-Kate finally admitted. "Especially for sitting at the cool table without her. Now I feel awful—and it's all my fault."

"Cheer up, Mary-Kate," Amanda said. "Ashley probably forgot about the whole thing. What's she doing now?"

"Throwing darts at my picture," Mary-Kate said glumly.

"Oh," Amanda said.

Mary-Kate and Amanda watched some more boys pass by.

"I want to find the perfect boy for Ashley to kiss," Mary-Kate said, thinking out loud. "You know, someone she's comfortable with. Someone who's almost like a friend."

Just then she found her answer walking down the street—Max and Brian!

"That's it!" Mary-Kate exclaimed, pointing to the boys.

"Max and Brian?" Amanda shrieked. "Are you for real?"

Mary-Kate jumped up from the stoop and waved to her friends. Max and Brian were carrying their softball equipment.

"Hey, guys," Mary-Kate said.

"Why weren't you at softball practice?" Max asked.

"Something came up," Mary-Kate replied. "Something important. Did I miss anything?"

Brian nodded. "Ben Fahey got his catcher's mask caught on his retainer."

"Ouch," Mary-Kate said, wincing.

Max gave a wave. "Oh, well. See you in school tomorrow."

"Yeah," Brian echoed. "See you."

Max and Brian began to walk away. Mary-Kate knew she had to do something. Now.

She jumped in front of them.

"Wait, you guys!" Mary-Kate called. "Amanda and I were just sort of hanging around. Would you like to do something?"

Max and Brian looked at each other.

"What sort of 'something'?" Max asked.

Mary-Kate thought fast. "How about a mean game of Nintendo?" she suggested. "Up in my attic. I'll spring for the sodas."

"It's a deal," Brian said. He paused. "As long as we get to win."

Mary-Kate snorted. "Dream on."

"I think I'll miss this," Amanda said. She gave Mary-Kate the thumbs-up. "Good luck."

"Thanks," Mary-Kate replied. "Come on, you guys." Let's go."

She turned around and ran up the stoop.

It's an awesome plan, she thought, crossing her fingers.

Ashley gets to kiss a guy. And I get to help my sister—and myself.

I just hope it works!

CHAPTER THIRTEEN

"Having fun, Ashley?" Mary-Kate asked as she entered the attic. The room had a sofa, a small TV, and a telescope by the window.

There were also posters of famous superstars and athletes. But this time, the poster of Sammy Sosa was replaced by a dart-filled photograph of Mary-Kate.

"As a matter of fact, I am," Ashley replied. She picked up another dart and flung it at the picture. It landed in the middle of her sister's nose with a thwack.

"Ye-es!" Ashley cried. "Bull's-eye!"

Mary-Kate tilted her head and studied the picture. "You know, that's a picture of you," she pointed out.

Ugh. Ashley scowled. Her sister was right.

"What do you want now?" she asked.

"Ashley," Mary-Kate said slowly. "I have decided to solve your problem!"

"Solve my problem?" Ashley repeated. "What do you mean?"

Mary-Kate didn't answer. She simply put two fingers to her lips and gave a loud, shrill whistle.

Max and Brian walked through the door and into the attic.

"Hi, Ashley," Brian said. He took a long swig from a soda can.

"What's up?" Max asked.

"Okay, Ashley," Mary-Kate said. She pointed to Max and Brian. "Pick a guy. Any guy."

"What for?" Ashley asked.

"To kiss!" Mary-Kate answered. She beamed at her sister.

Ashley stared at Mary-Kate. She couldn't believe what she had just heard. "What did you say?"

"Wait a minute!" Max cried. "You told us we were going to play Nintendo!"

"I lied," Mary-Kate said.

"Why would I kiss them?" Ashley asked.

"Come on, Ashley," Mary-Kate said. "If you kiss a boy, my kiss will be old news. Everybody will think *you're* the cool one. We'll be even."

"Not if I kiss one of these guys," Ashley said.

"I can't kiss her!" Max cried. "I've known her since she was a little kid."

Ashley glanced over at Brian. He was spraying his mouth with a tiny can of breath spray.

"Well, she's not a little kid anymore," Brian said. He swaggered over to Ashley and winked. "Ready when you are, babe."

"Look, Brian," Ashley said with a sigh, "why don't you call me when your permanent teeth come in?"

"Huh?" Brian said.

"Let's go, Brian," Max grumbled. "Who needs to be trashed like this?"

Mary-Kate ran to the door and hustled her friends out.

"Thanks, guys," Mary-Kate said in a low voice. "Sorry it didn't work out."

"You have my number if you change your mind," Brian called to Ashley from the doorway.

Ashley rolled her eyes.

Mary-Kate turned around slowly. "I was just trying to help," she said in a small voice.

Ashley could almost feel the steam coming out of her ears. She was never so mad in her life.

"Help?" Ashley cried. "I don't need your help. I can find my own guy to kiss!"

"That's cool, Ashley," Mary-Kate said brightly.

"But in the meantime, why don't we go downstairs and bake some chocolate chip cookies? It will be just like old times—you heat 'em, I eat 'em!"

"No!" Ashley snapped.

Mary-Kate's shoulders drooped.

"Fine," she finally said. "I was just trying to make things better between us, that's all." She slowly walked out of the room.

"My own guy to kiss," Ashley repeated to herself when the door closed behind Mary-Kate. "That's what I need. A guy I choose myself."

A smile spread across her face.

"And I know just where to find him."

CHAPTER
FOURTEEN

"I know this test was difficult," Kevin said to his class that afternoon. "But you should have done better. I mean, every senior on campus probably has my old exams on file."

Carrie held her breath as Kevin handed back their tests. She had waited all weekend for this moment—the moment when she would find out if she aced the test or blew it!

"Carrie," Kevin said as he handed back her test.

"Yes?" Carrie asked, her voice cracking. She picked up the paper and stared at it.

She got an A!

Yes! she thought. *My hard work has finally paid off!*

"What did you get, Carrie?" Paul asked. He leaned over and peered at Carrie's test. "Oh . . . you got an A. Congratulations."

"Maybe I should have a sleepover at the professor's, too." Brett snickered.

Carrie felt her face turn red. She spun around and glared at him.

"Get a life," she snapped. "I worked hard for this. I was up all night!"

"I'm sure you were." Paul laughed. "A pizza with everything on it goes a long, long way!"

Carrie's mouth tightened as she heard some other students laugh.

It was time to set the record straight!

"Hey, look," she told the class, "I do not have to date a professor to get a good grade. I earned this A."

"Professor," she called out to him, "help me out here, will you?"

Kevin leaned against his desk. He folded his arms and shrugged.

"No comment," he said.

"Whoa!" Brett cried. "This is getting intense!"

Carrie's jaw dropped as she stared at Kevin.

"No comment?" she gasped.

"No comment," Kevin repeated.

He smiled at the class. "See you tomorrow. And

don't forget to read the next chapter."

The students stood up and headed for the door.

"Wait!" Carrie called to her classmates. "This isn't right! I really earned this A!"

Paul winked at her as he passed by.

"I'm sure you did, Carrie!" he said. Then he and Brett hurried out the door, laughing.

"That does it!" Carrie said. She marched over to Kevin's desk.

"How could you do that, Professor?" she demanded. "Now they think I got that A because of the other night."

"Hey," Kevin said. "What do you care what they think? After all, your personal life is none of their business . . . right?"

Carrie blushed as she heard the familiar words.

"Look." She sighed. "I don't care if the class thinks I'm dating you. I just don't want them to think I'm dating you for a grade."

"And as a professor, I don't want them to think I'm dating you . . . period!" Kevin said firmly.

"Now I understand," Carrie said. She looked down at her test paper and sighed. "You know, this is my first A since I came back to school. But now it's ruined."

Kevin shook his head.

"Judging from your work, Carrie," he said, "I think this will be the first A of many!"

"You think so, Professor Burke?" Carrie asked. She beamed at him.

"Oh, absolutely." Kevin smiled. "Your understanding of crystals is—crystal clear!"

"Thanks," Carrie said, smiling.

But she was still worried. "The class is going to think that I got them all for the same reason, Professor. What are we going to do?"

Kevin scratched his chin. "Well . . . I guess there's only one thing left to do," he said.

"What?" Carrie asked.

"We have to break up!" Kevin decided.

"Oooh—a breakup!" Carrie said. "That's good!"

"And it should be ugly," Kevin said. "And very public so everyone can hear it!"

"Awesome!" Carrie agreed. "I'll tell you what. I'll dump you tomorrow right in front of the whole class."

"Why wait?" Kevin asked. "If I know my students, they're probably still hanging around outside the classroom."

Carrie glanced at the door. "No way!"

"You don't think so?" Kevin said, a sly twinkle in his eye. "Just watch this."

Kevin cleared his throat. Then he began to yell.
"What do you mean, you want to stop dating me?"

Carrie's eyes popped wide open. He sounded so convincing!

"Go ahead," Kevin whispered. "Your line."

"Oh . . . yeah," Carrie said. She thought fast. Then she began to yell, too.

"Because this A is a joke! I should have gotten an A plus!"

"An A plus?" Kevin shouted.

Carrie grinned. She was getting into this. "And another thing," she yelled. "I hate your taste in pizza!"

"What's wrong with my taste in pizza?" Kevin shouted back.

"Extra cheese and pepperoni make me gag!" Carrie screamed at the top of her lungs.

Kevin laughed silently as he gave her a quick thumbs-up sign.

Carrie went on. "As far as I'm concerned, Professor Burke, it's over. Over!"

Carrie spun around on her platform heel and stomped toward the door. When she swung it open, Paul and Brett fell into the classroom.

Kevin was right. They were there all the time!

"Do you want something?" Carrie frowned

down at Paul and Brett.

"Yeah," Paul said, looking up from the floor. He gave Carrie a weak grin. "I want to know . . . what's wrong with pepperoni?"

CHAPTER FIFTEEN

"When is this stupid math lesson going to be over?" Ashley whispered to herself as she peeked into the living room.

Mary-Kate was sitting on the sofa beside Taylor Donovan, her math tutor. And Ashley's major crush.

Taylor would be perfect for Ashley's first kiss. If only she could figure out how to manage it.

Then Ashley heard the magic words . . .

"I've got to get going, Mary-Kate," Taylor said as he closed his book. "Be sure to work on your decimals for next time."

"Decimals?" Mary-Kate groaned. "You're killing me here, Taylor."

"Sorry," Taylor said. "But if I want my ten bucks

for tutoring, I have to say that sort of stuff."

"Got it," Mary-Kate said.

Ashley ducked behind the door frame as Mary-Kate ran up the stairs. Her sister always left the living room before Taylor did.

She peeked into the living room again. Taylor was just getting up from the sofa.

"Alone at last," Ashley whispered.

She could hear Carrie washing the snack dishes in the kitchen. Mary-Kate was upstairs in their room.

It was time to put her plan into action.

Ready or not, here I come, Ashley thought. She straightened her pink sweater and threw back her shoulders. Then she strolled into the living room.

"Oh, Taylor," she greeted him. "I'm glad I caught you. Is that a new shirt?"

"A new shirt?" Taylor said, wrinkling his nose. "No. Why?"

"Oh, I don't know," Ashley said. "It's just . . . so clean."

Shrugging, Taylor sniffed an armpit.

"Anyway," Ashley went on, "before you leave, could you help me with this one math problem?"

"It must be a tough one if you need help, Ashley," Taylor said. "You're a real math whiz."

Walking over to the coffee table, Ashley grinned.

She picked up one of Mary-Kate's books and opened it.

"Oh, it is," Ashley said. "It's uh . . . this one here. Problem number twelve."

Ashley peered over Taylor's shoulder while he studied the page. If she wanted to kiss him she would have to act fast. She would have to surprise him.

Ashley began to move closer . . . and closer . . . and—

"I got it!" Taylor shouted. He sat up quickly.

CRASH!

"OW!" they both shouted as Taylor's head bumped into Ashley's chin.

Ashley saw a zillion stars as she rubbed her sore chin.

"Ashley, are you okay?" Taylor said. He put his hands on Ashley's shoulders.

Ashley frowned.

"Yeah, I'm fine," she said. "Are you okay?"

"Yeah," Taylor said. "But you kind of hit my head."

"I-I was trying to see the problem," Ashley explained.

But the real problem now was that she felt like a jerk.

"Oh, okay," Taylor said. He sat back down and pointed to the book. "If you just convert the decimal into a fraction, you can do a straight multiplication."

"Oh, right," Ashley said. "That's easy. Thanks, Taylor."

"No problem," Taylor said. "And sorry about smacking into you. See you."

Ashley watched as Taylor walked out of the house.

I can't do anything right, Ashley thought in disgust.

She stomped angrily into the kitchen. She walked past Carrie and began pulling out pots, pans, and bags of sugar and flour.

"Ashley?" Carrie asked. "What are you doing?"

"Baking!" Ashley snapped.

"An hour before dinner?" Carrie asked. "How come?"

Ashley slammed a mixing bowl onto the counter.

"Because it's the only thing I know how to do well, that's why!" she muttered. "I can't play softball, I can't throw a decent sleepover, and I never even kissed a boy!"

Carrie leaned over the counter. "Kiss? Ashley, let's start from the beginning here. What happened?"

Ashley heaved a big sigh.

"At my sleepover, during Truth or Dare, Mary-Kate said she kissed a boy," Ashley explained. "And now all my friends want to hang out with her!"

Carrie's eyes opened wide. "Mary-Kate kissed a boy?"

"Believe me," Ashley groaned. "No one was as surprised as I was. Especially when I found out that Mary-Kate kept the whole thing a secret from me."

"I guess everybody has secrets," Carrie said with a smile. "Even twins."

"That's only part of the problem," Ashley went on. "Now I have to kiss a boy so we're even. So things will be like they used to be."

"Wow," Carrie said. "That *is* a problem."

"Tell me about it," Ashley muttered. She reached into the refrigerator and pulled out a handful of lemons.

"You know," Carrie said, "I remember my first kiss. I was fourteen."

"Did you say *fourteen?*" Ashley gasped. "You waited that long to kiss a boy?"

Carrie nodded. "Yup. His name was Philip McKenna. We rode the school bus together for six months before we kissed."

Ashley put the lemons on the counter. "What was it like?" she asked.

"The bus ride?" Carrie asked. "Bumpy."

"No, Carrie, the kiss. Tell me about the kiss," Ashley urged. "And don't leave out a single detail!"

"Okay, okay," Carrie said. Her eyes turned toward the ceiling as she tried to remember. "It was a rainy day. We were huddled under his umbrella waiting for the bus."

"Yeah? Yeah?" Ashley said. "Then what happened?"

"He leaned in, his face dripping wet," Carrie went on. "Then . . . he kissed me."

"Wow," Ashley sighed. "How did it feel?"

"It was beautiful," Carrie said. She paused. "Then he dropped my books in the mud."

"You remember all that?" Ashley asked. "I mean . . . when you were fourteen it was— "

"The Stone Age?" Carrie joked.

"No!" Ashley said. "It was just a while back, that's all."

"I know." Carrie smiled. "But you never forget a kiss that means something. We really liked each other, and we didn't do it to prove anything to anybody."

Ashley stared down at the counter. "So it wasn't because of some stupid game, huh?"

"No way," Carrie said. "Your first kiss should be for yourself. Not for your friends."

Ashley nodded slowly. "Or for my sister."

"You got it," Carrie said.

Ashley smiled. Why didn't she go to Carrie with her problem in the first place?

"And as for Mary-Kate keeping a secret from you, forget about it," Carrie said. "One of these days you might have a secret you'll want to keep from Mary-Kate."

Ashley gave it a thought. Then she grinned.

"I already do!" she said.

"What?" Carrie asked.

Lifting the mixing bowl, Ashley smiled proudly.

"My recipe for Luscious Lemon Squares. Just let Mary-Kate try to get *that* out of me!"

CHAPTER SIXTEEN

"So how come you're so nice to me all of a sudden?" Mary-Kate asked Ashley as they headed to their classroom the next morning.

"It's a secret!" Ashley joked.

"Well, if you ask me, it's a relief," Amanda said, walking behind them. "There's nothing worse than fighting twins. It's unnatural!"

The girls were about to turn the corner when Jennifer Dilber stepped in front of them.

"Hi, guys," Jennifer Dilber said. She was wearing a suede jacket with matching pants and lots of makeup.

"Hey, Jennifer," Mary-Kate said. "What's new?"

Jennifer glanced from Mary-Kate to Ashley.

"Actually, I want to talk to your sister."

Mary-Kate's eyes opened wide. This was a switch!

"Me?" Ashley asked. "What for?"

Jennifer looked around the hallway. Then she lowered her voice.

"This morning while I was putting on my makeup I made a very important decision," Jennifer declared.

"Don't tell me," Ashley said. "You're switching from purple eye shadow to green!"

"No!" Jennifer sounded impatient. "Somewhere between the lipstick and the mascara, I decided that today would be the day!"

"For what?" Amanda asked.

"The day I would finally kiss a boy!" Jennifer announced excitedly.

Here we go again, Mary-Kate thought.

"What made you decide that?" Ashley asked.

"Easy," Jennifer said. "I realized that if someone like your sister could kiss a boy, anybody can do it!"

Mary-Kate narrowed her eyes. "Gee, thanks, Jennifer."

Jennifer waved the girls into a corner.

"Okay, here's the plan," Jennifer whispered. "A bunch of ninth-grade boys always play basketball in the park after school."

"So you want to kiss them?" Amanda asked.

"Du-uh!" Jennifer groaned. "What else would I want to do? Shoot hoops?"

"You bet!" Mary-Kate nodded. Shooting hoops was much more fun than kissing!

"But they're ninth-grade boys," Amanda said, wide-eyed. *"Teenagers!"*

"I know," Jennifer said. "That makes it even more cool."

Mary-Kate watched as Jennifer dug into her backpack for a small paper bag. Then she pulled out a tube of lipstick.

"See?" Jennifer said. "I bought this on the way to school. It's called Very Violet. Guaranteed not to kiss off."

"You bought a special lipstick for a stupid kiss?" Mary-Kate asked. "What for?"

"Oh, Mary-Kate, Mary-Kate," Jennifer said with a laugh. "You're so funny, acting like this is no big deal."

"Come on, Jennifer," Ashley said. "If you want to kiss a boy today, what does that have to do with us?"

"Because I know you want to kiss a boy, too, Ashley," Jennifer said. "Amanda told me."

Ashley looked sideways at Amanda. "Oh, she did, did she?"

Amanda threw her hands in the air.

"I couldn't control myself, Ashley!" she sputtered. "I love tacos, too!"

Jennifer tapped her chin as she stared at Amanda. "And I happen to know that you also want to kiss a boy, Amanda."

"I do?" Amanda gulped. Then she smiled nervously. "Oh—yeah, sure I do!"

Mary-Kate glanced over at Ashley. Maybe this was just what Ashley needed to feel cool.

"Come on, Ashley," Mary-Kate said. "Now's your big chance. Do it."

"Nope," Ashley said, shaking her head.

"What?" Mary-Kate asked.

"I don't want to do it," Ashley explained. Then she smiled. "I want my first kiss to be special. That's why I want to wait until I can kiss a boy I really like."

"You what?" Mary-Kate sputtered.

"But, Ashley," Jennifer cried. "Waiting for the right boy could take forever."

"Maybe," Ashley said. "But I'd rather wait for one kiss that really counts."

Mary-Kate, Amanda, and Jennifer stared silently at Ashley.

"Wow, Ashley," Jennifer finally said. "That was so . . . so mature! I mean, I didn't think of it that way . . . "

"Slow down now, Jennifer," Mary-Kate said, her hands on her hips. "A few seconds ago you were ready to kiss the entire junior high school basketball team."

"That was five minutes ago," Jennifer said with a wave of her hand. "Ashley's got a point. Good things are worth waiting for!"

Jennifer turned away from Mary-Kate. She placed her hand on Ashley's shoulder.

"Let's all meet after school," Jennifer suggested. "But not to kiss a boy."

"What should we do instead?" Amanda asked.

"I know!" Ashley said. "Let's cut out Leonardo DiCaprio's face and paste it on Matt Damon's body!"

"Brilliant!" Jennifer cried.

Mary-Kate watched as Ashley walked down the hall with Jennifer and Amanda.

"Guys?" she called. "Does this mean I'm not the cool one anymore?"

CHAPTER SEVENTEEN

"Max, it's your bet," Mary-Kate said, peeking over her cards.

"Okay," Max said. "I'll see your two Oreo cookies and raise you a Chips Ahoy."

Mary-Kate watched as Max put his cookies in the middle of the kitchen table. They weren't the best poker players, but they sure had the tastiest poker chips!

"Come on, Brian," Carrie urged. She nodded over her cards. "The pot's getting stale."

Brian stared at his cards. Then he threw them down.

"So are my cards!" he groaned.

Just then Ashley entered through the back door

with Jennifer and Amanda.

"Hi, Carrie," Ashley said. "Hi, guys."

"Want to play poker?" Max asked.

Jennifer wrinkled her nose. "What's poker?"

Max sighed. "Never mind."

"Actually, we were just going up to the attic," Ashley said.

"Yeah!" Amanda said. She shifted the pile of teen magazines under her arm. "We've got some serious work to do."

"Homework?" Carrie asked.

Jennifer began to giggle. "Oh, sure. We're studying the history of teenage hunks!"

Mary-Kate watched as her sister left the kitchen with her friends. Ashley looked happy for the first time in days.

"Ashley's back in with her friends, huh?" Carrie asked, putting down her cards. "What happened?"

"Well," Mary-Kate said, "Jennifer wanted to go out and find boys to kiss, because that was the thing to do."

"Where was I?" Brian asked.

"Probably in the playground," Max joked.

"Then Ashley fed them some line about how she's waiting to kiss the right boy so it'll be really special," Mary-Kate went on.

"No kidding?" Carrie asked.

Mary-Kate nodded. "Yeah, and they bought it. Now Ashley's cool because she *hasn't* kissed a boy. Is that weird or what?"

"Totally," Carrie said.

Mary-Kate stared at her baby-sitter. There was something about the way she was smiling. Something sly . . .

"Carrie?" Mary-Kate smiled. "Did you have anything to do with this?"

"Who, me?" Carrie asked.

"Yeah, Carrie," Max said. "Come clean."

"Okay, okay," Carrie said. "I did offer Ashley a little kissing advice."

"You?" Brian cried.

"Hey," Carrie said. She bit into an Oreo cookie. "Poker isn't the only thing I'm good at."

Brian leaned back in his chair and heaved a big sigh. "It's all so clear now. Ashley's waiting for me!"

Mary-Kate held up her poker cards.

"So are we," she said. "Shut up and deal."

As Brian dealt the cards, Mary-Kate smiled to herself. Things would finally be back to normal again. Soon Ashley would be nagging her about her clothes, her messy side of the room, and her snoring. . . .

Mary-Kate could hardly wait!

Mary-Kate & Ashley's Scrapbook

It all started when Ashley
decided to have a sleepover
and invite Jennifer, the most
popular girl in school.

First Jennifer showed
us how to put on
makeup . . .

... then we called some guys.

The grossest part was when Amanda stuffed twenty marshmallows in her mouth!

But the biggest surprise was when Mary-Kate told
a secret that even Ashley didn't know!

For a while, Ashley was kind of upset with Mary-Kate . . .

... but it all worked out in the end. Now Mary-Kate is back to playing cards with the boys—and Ashley is back to dreaming about them ...

... but we'll still be best friends forever!

PSST! Take a sneak peek
at

One Twin Too Many

"And here's another thing Pokey and I have in common!" Ashley announced to her sister. The girls were lounging in their bedroom. Ashley lay on her flower-print bedspread, writing in her notebook.

I bet she's writing about Pokey Valentine again, Mary-Kate thought. Pokey was a very cute boy in the twins' class at school. Ashley had a major crush on him.

But Mary-Kate knew something her sister didn't know. A few days earlier, Pokey had asked Mary-Kate out—not Ashley!

"Don't you want to know what it is?" Ashley prompted.

"Okay," Mary-Kate said with a nervous gulp. "What do you and Pokey have in common?"

"Both our names end in E-Y!" Ashley gushed.

Oh, man, Mary-Kate thought. *How am I going to tell her the truth now?*

She's getting more and more of a crush on him!

"Uh, you know, Ashley," Mary-Kate said cautiously, "I wouldn't get too carried away with him. I mean, maybe you should take things slow."

Ashley tossed her blond hair over her shoulder with a flick of her hand. "Oh, I think I'm mature enough not to rush into anything," she informed Mary-Kate coolly. Then she whirled around and quickly showed her sister the notebook she'd been writing in. "Which looks better? Ashley Valentine? Or Ashley Burke-Valentine?"

Mary-Kate rolled her eyes. "Marriage?" she exclaimed. "You're planning to marry him?"

"Well, it wasn't my idea," Ashley argued. "We were talking about weird names the other day, and he said, 'Try living with Pokey for a while.'"

"So?" Mary-Kate asked.

"So think about it, Mary-Kate!" Mary cried. "He asked me to think about living with his name! Doesn't that sound like a proposal of marriage to you?"

"Not exactly," Mary-Kate shook her head.

Especially not when he's asked me *out for a date!* she thought.

Mary-Kate's throat closed up. Her stomach

turned over. She felt worse and worse.

Ashley was going to be so upset!

I've got to find some way to tell her, Mary-Kate decided. *This can't go on!*

But before she thought of a way to bring it up, Carrie poked her head into the twins' room. "It's your turn to set the table tonight, Ashley," Carrie announced.

Ashley hopped up right away.

"My pleasure," she said happily. "Isn't life glorious?"

"Boy, she's in a good mood," Carrie commented when Ashley was gone.

"Not for long," Mary-Kate muttered.

"Oh—you saw dinner, huh?" Carrie guessed. "I swear it looked better on the box!"

"I'm not talking about dinner," Mary-Kate said. "It's . . ." She trailed off.

Carrie sat down on Mary-Kate's bed. "Okay," she said. "Out with it. What's the matter?"

"I've got a problem," Mary-Kate admitted. "A big problem. About Ashley."

Carrie smiled.

"Oh, I get it," she said. "You're probably feeling a little jealous because Ashley might have a boyfriend. But don't worry—your time will come."

"It already has!" Mary-Kate blurted out.

"Really? Who is he?" Carrie scooted in closer to hear the news.

Mary-Kate gulped.

"Pokey."

"Pokey?" Carrie's eyes opened wide. "Ashley's Pokey?"

Mary-Kate slapped the bed in frustration. "How many Pokeys do you know?" she cried. "Yes—Ashley's Pokey! He invited me over to his house for a date. What am I going to do?"

"I think you know what you have to do," Carrie counseled her. "You have to tell Ashley."

Mary-Kate's shoulders slumped. Sure, she did know it. But it was going to be hard. So hard.

"Can I do it from the pay phone on the corner?" Mary-Kate asked. " I mean, Ashley is scrawny—but she's got a great left hook!"

Carrie laughed and put her arm around Mary-Kate's shoulder. "Just do it," Carrie advised. "The sooner the better."

"Oh boy," Mary-Kate sighed. Her stomach turned over again.

She knew she had to do it—just tell Ashley the truth and get it over with.

But what she didn't know was this: How mad was Ashley going to be when she found out?

OFFICIAL RULES

1. No purchase necessary

2. To enter complete the official entry form or hand print your name, address, and phone number along with the words "*Two of a Kind™* Visit-to-the-Hollywood-Set-and-Meet-Mary-Kate-and-Ashley Sweepstakes" on a 3 x 5 card and mail to: *Two of a Kind™* Visit-to-the-Hollywood-Set-and-Meet-Mary-Kate-and-Ashley Sweepstakes, c/o HarperCollins, Attn.: Department AW, 10 E. 53rd Street, New York, NY 10022. Entries must be received by April 31, 1999. Enter as often as you wish, but each entry must be mailed separately. One entry per envelope. No facsimiles accepted. Partially completed, illegible or mechanically reproduced entries will not be accepted. Sponsors are not responsible for lost, late, mutilated, illegible, stolen, postage due, incomplete or misdirected entries. All entries become the property of HarperCollins and will not be returned.

3. Sweepstakes open to all legal residents of the United States, who are between the ages of five and twelve by April 31, 1999 excluding employees and immediate family members of HarperCollins, Warner Bros. Television, Parachute Properties and Parachute Press Inc., and their respective subsidiaries and affiliates, officers, directors, shareholders, employees, agents, attorneys and other representatives (individually and collectively "Parachute"), Dualstar Entertainment Group, Inc. and its subsidiaries and affiliates, officers, directors, shareholders, employees, agents, attorneys and other representatives (individually and collectively "Dualstar"), and their respective parent companies, affiliates, subsidiaries, advertising, promotion and fulfillment agencies, and the persons with whom each of the above are domiciled. Offer void where prohibited or restricted.

4. Odds of winning depend on total number of entries received. Approximately 100,000 entry forms distributed. All prizes will be awarded. Winners will be randomly drawn on or about May 5, 1999 by representatives of HarperCollins, whose decisions are final. Potential winners will be notified by mail and a parent or guardian of the potential winner will be required to sign and return an affidavit of eligibility and release of liability within 14 days of notification. Failure to return affidavit within time period will disqualify winner and another winner will be chosen. By acceptance of prize, winner consents to the use of his or her name, photographs, likeness, and personal information by HarperCollins, Parachute, Dualstar, Warner for publicity and advertising, purposes without further compensation except where prohibited.

5. One (1) Grand Prize Winner will receive a visit to the *Two of a Kind™* set, where they will meet Mary-Kate and Ashley Olsen. HarperCollins, Parachute, and Dualstar, reserve the right to substitute another prize of equal or of greater value in the event that the winner is unable to receive the prize for any reason. All expenses not stated are at the winner's sole expense.

5a. HarperEntertainment will provide the contest winner and one parent or legal guardian with round-trip coach air transportation from major airport nearest winner to Los Angeles, CA, visit to the set of *Two of a Kind™* and standard hotel accommodations for a two night stay. Trip must be taken within one year from the date prize is awarded. All additional expenses including taxes, meals, and incidentals are the responsibility of the prize winner. Airline, hotel and other travel arrangements will be made by HarperCollins in its discretion. HarperCollins reserves the right to substitute a cash payment of $2,000 for the Grand Prize. Travel and use of hotel are at risk of winner and HarperCollins does not assume any liability.

6. Only one prize will be awarded per individual, family, or household. Prizes are nontransferable and cannot be sold or redeemed for cash. No cash substitute is available. Any federal, state or local taxes are the responsibility of the winner.

7. Additional terms: By participating, entrants agree a) to the official rules and decisions of the judges which will be final in all respects; and b) to release, discharge and hold harmless HarperCollins, Parachute, Dualstar, Warner Bros. and their affiliates, subsidiaries and advertising promotion agencies from and against any and all liability or damages associated with acceptance, use or misuse of any prize received in this sweepstakes.

8. To obtain the name of the winners, please send your request and a self-addressed stamped envelope (excluding residents of Vermont and Washington) to *Two of a Kind™* Visit-to-the-Hollywood-Set-and-Meet-Mary-Kate-and-Ashley Sweepstakes. c/o HarperCollins, 10 E. 53rd Street, New York, NY 10022.

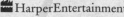

Don't Miss Mary-Kate & Ashley
in their 2 newest videos!

Available Now Only on Video.

High Above Hollywood Mary-Kate & Ashley Are Playing Matchmakers!
Check Them Out in Their Coolest New Movie

Mary-Kate Olsen

Ashley Olsen

Billboard DAD

One's a surfer. The other's a high diver. When these two team up to find a new love for their single Dad by taking out a personals ad on a billboard in the heart of Hollywood, it's a fun-loving, eye-catching California adventure gone wild!

Now on Video!

DUALSTAR VIDEO

Two Times the Fun!
Two Times the Excitement!
Two Times the Adventure!

Check Out All Six *You're Invited* Video Titles...

...And All Four Feature-Length Movies!

And Look for Mary-Kate & Ashley's
Adventure Video Series.

It doesn't matter if you live around the corner...
or around the world....
If you are a fan of Mary-Kate and Ashley Olsen,
you should be a member of

Mary-Kate + Ashley's Fun Club™

Here's what you get
Our Funzine™
- An autographed color photo
Two black and white individual photos
A full sized color poster
An official Fun Club™ membership card
A Fun Club™ School folder
Two special Fun Club™ surprises
Fun Club™ Collectible Catalog
Plus a Fun Club™ box to keep everything in.

To join Mary-Kate + Ashley's Fun Club™, fill out the form below
and send it along with

U.S. Residents	$17.00
Canadian Residents	$22.00 (US Funds only)
International Residents	$27.00 (US Funds only)

Mary-Kate + Ashley's Fun Club™
859 Hollywood Way, Suite 275
Burbank, CA 91505

Name:_____

Address:_____

City:_____ St:_____ Zip:_____

Phone: (_____) _____

E-Mail:_____

Check us out on the web at
www.marykateandashley.com